WORSE THAN ROTTEN, RALPH

For Katherine,

Jack Gantos

Text by Jack Gantos   Art by Nicole Rubel

Houghton Mifflin Company Boston

To Carew

Library of Congress Cataloging in Publication Data

Gantos, Jack
  Worse than rotten, Ralph.

  SUMMARY: Rotten Ralph makes an earnest attempt
at good behavior but is enticed, not too reluctantly,
into a series of misadventures by some ruffian alley
cats.
  [1. Cats—Fiction. 2. Behavior—Fiction]
I. Rubel, Nicole.
II. Title.
PZ7.G15334Wo   [E]   78-6512
ISBN 0-395-27106-1

**The character of Rotten Ralph was originally
created by Nicole Rubel and Jack Gantos.**

ISBN: 0-395-27106-1 Reinforced Edition
ISBN: 0-395-32919-1 Sandpiper Paperbound Edition

Printed in the United States of America
WOZ 10

One morning when Sarah woke up, Rotten Ralph
was swinging on her chandelier.

"I have to run some errands today," Sarah said as she tied a pretty ribbon around Ralph's neck. "While I'm away I want you to behave."

When Sarah left the house Ralph tried to find
something nice to do.
"I'd rather be fishing," he moaned while
watching Sarah's fish.
Instead, he fed them breakfast.

Staying out of trouble made him tired so he
decided to take a nap. But while he was lying
in his hammock a tough alley cat came by.
"Hey softy," he called to Ralph, "why don't
you stop sleeping your life away."
"Leave me alone," replied Ralph. "I'm trying
to behave."
"Why I bet you don't even know how to be
rotten," said the alley cat.
"That's not true," said Ralph.
"Prove it," sneered the alley cat.
Ralph slowly got up from the hammock.

The alley cat took Ralph to meet his gang
of friends.

"I dare you to help us push over some trash
cans," said the leader.

"I don't want to cause trouble," Ralph replied.
Still he took off his bow. Then he gently
pushed over one can.

The alley cats had a great time.

"To the park!" ordered the leader.

Ralph and the alley cats climbed up into a
tree and knocked hats off the passers-by.

Ralph knocked off almost as many hats as the
other cats.

SEE THE WILD WEST SHOW!

SPOT

Afterward the cats leaped out of the tree
as though they were a pack of tigers. They
crept along the ground and soon sneaked up on
some nice cats.

"Growl," roared the alley cats.

"Growwlll," roared Ralph louder than anyone else.

The nice cats cried and ran away.

The alley cats couldn't think of anything
else to do.
Then Ralph said, "If you dare to follow me I'll show you
some real fun."
"We can do anything a soft house cat can do,"
scoffed the leader. They followed Ralph downtown.

They went into Frankenstein's Costume Shop and
tried on all the costumes.

"This is more fun than chasing rats,"
said the leader.

"You haven't seen anything yet," boasted Ralph.

"I'll eat you alive," growled Frankenstein
as he chased them around the shop.

Then they ran through Pierre's Poodle Parlor.

The poodles screamed and ran away.

"When I catch you I'll clip off your tails!"

threatened Pierre.

"Charge!" shouted Ralph as the alley cats ran
into a bakery. Rotten Ralph took a pie and threw
it in the leader's face.
Immediately a pie fight began.
"Get out of here or I'll turn you into
gingerbread cats!" shouted the owner.

The alley cats were beginning to grow tired
but Ralph took them home anyway.
"Let's play follow the leader," he announced.
"I'm the leader."
Rotten Ralph took them into Sarah's room. They
jumped up and down on her bed until it broke.

"Everyone has to paint wild pictures on the wall," Ralph declared.

He gave them Sarah's paints and soon the walls were dripping with bright colors.

They were banging pots and pans together when
Sarah returned home.

"You nasty cats!" she shouted.

"Leave my Ralph alone!"

She picked up a broom and chased them out the
back door while Ralph hid behind a chair.

"You poor thing. You must have been so frightened," Sarah said while brushing Ralph's messy fur. "It wasn't very nice of those horrible alley cats to lead you astray and make you do so many rotten things."

Sarah loved Ralph very much.

He sighed. "I can't be all rotten," Ralph said to himself.

Still, he hoped the alley cats would dare to
call him a softy again.